The Amish Project

by Jessica Dickey

A SAMUEL FRENCH ACTING EDITION

SAMUEL FRENCH

FOUNDED 1830

NEW YORK HOLLYWOOD LONDON TORONTO

SAMUELFRENCH.COM

ISBN 978-0-573-69888-0   Printed in U.S.A.   #29666

MUSIC USE NOTE

Licensees are solely responsible for obtaining formal written permission from copyright owners to use copyrighted music in the performance of this play and are strongly cautioned to do so. If no such permission is obtained by the licensee, then the licensee must use only original music that the licensee owns and controls. Licensees are solely responsible and liable for all music clearances and shall indemnify the copyright owners of the play and their licensing agent, Samuel French, Inc., against any costs, expenses, losses and liabilities arising from the use of music by licensees.

IMPORTANT BILLING AND CREDIT
REQUIREMENTS

All producers of *THE AMISH PROJECT must* give credit to the Author of the Play in all programs distributed in connection with performances of the Play, and in all instances in which the title of the Play appears for the purposes of advertising, publicizing or otherwise exploiting the Play and/ or a production. The name of the Author *must* appear on a separate line on which no other name appears, immediately following the title and *must* appear in size of type not less than fifty percent of the size of the title type.

In addition the following credit *must* be given in all programs and publicity information distributed in association with this piece:

The Amish Project was originally presented in the New York International Fringe Festival in association with Nora Productions, and further developed and produced by Cherry Lane Theater, Angelina Fiordellisi, Artistic Director.

World premiere produced by Rattlestick Playwrights Theater in association with Nora Productions.

These productions were directed by Sarah Cameron Sunde.

The Amish Project was first produced at the New York International Fringe Festival on August 8, 2008 in the Players Loft. The performance was directed by Sarah Cameron Sunde, assisted by Lillian Vince, with sets by Lauren Helpern and sound by Austin Bunn. The production stage manager was Emily Ballou. The cast was as follows:

VELDA, ANNA, CAROL STUCKEY, BILL NORTH, SHERRY LOCAL,
    AMERICA, EDDIE STUCKEY . . . . Jessica Dickey

The Amish Project recieved its Off Broadway premiere produced by the Rattlestick Playwrights at the Rattlestick Playwrights Theater on June 10, 2009. The performance was directed by Sarah Cameron Sunde, assisted by Lillian Vince, with sets and costume by Lauren Helpern, lights by Nicole Pearce, and sound by Jill BC Du Boff. The production manager was Natalie Robin and the stage manager was Kelly Schaffer. The cast was as follows:

VELDA, ANNA, CAROL STUCKEY, BILL NORTH, SHERRY LOCAL,
    AMERICA, EDDIE STUCKEY . . . . Jessica Dickey

CHARACTERS

ANNA – Amish girl, age 14. Victim of the shooting.

CAROL STUCKEY – Widow of the gunman, age 31. English/non-Amish.

VELDA – Amish girl, age 6. Sister of Anna. Victim of the shooting.

BILL NORTH – English/non-Amish man, 50s. Scholar and professor on
    Amish culture, as well as friend and spokesman to several Amish
    families affected by the shooting.

AMERICA – Hispanic girl, age 16. Pregnant. Works in the local grocery
    store.

EDDIE STUCKEY – The gunman of schoolhouse shooting, age 33. Eng-
    lish/non-Amish. Killed himself at the end of the schoolhouse
    attack.

SHERRY LOCAL – English/non-Amish woman, age 53. Resident of
    Nickel Mines, PA.

A single actress performs all of the roles in the play. Distinctions between
characters are made by changes in the tonal qualities and pitch of the
actress' voice; through her stance, posture, and gesture. She glides flu-
idly from one personality to the next.

**This play is a fictional exploration of a real event that took place on
October 2, 2006 in Nickel Mines, PA. Characters are entirely fictional
and are not meant to represent real people.**

SETTING

The set should be very sparse; it should represent the natural beauty and simplicity of the Amish country of rural Pennsylvania.

COSTUMING

The basic costume is that of a traditional, Old Order Amish girl – a blue cotton dress that falls just below the knee, a white apron, stockings, and functional, black walking shoes. She should wear her hair in a neat bun beneath the traditional white bonnet. This clothing is constant throughout the play and is the primary uniform. Every character in *The Amish Project* wears the ethnic garb of the Amish girls murdered in the Nickel Mines schoolhouse shooting.

PRODUCTION NOTES

Several transitions have been listed throughout the script. These are simply moments when a sound cue or pause in the action may enhance the storytelling.

The character of Eddie should feel present onstage before his actual entrance in the text, and I encourage you to find the moments he is there. Additionally, Aaron, the invisible Amish father, is a powerful presence in the play, particularly for Bill North; the more the audience can feel him too, the better.

In general, I have chosen not to include any blocking from the original production. My hope is that the text will enable each production to discover its own vocabulary for the telling of the story.

And finally, each character of *The Amish Project* has a very good sense of humor. I hope you will struggle valiantly to let that be with them on stage.

A NOTE FROM THE PLAYWRIGHT

I have learned through the making of *The Amish Project* that the boundary between fact and fiction is a fraught one; it feels appropriate to open a window into my negotiation with that boundary.

The facts: *The Amish Project* is a fictional exploration of a true event. I absorbed a great deal about the Nickel Mines shooting just from watching the news when it occurred, and so in preparation for writing the play, I focused my attention on researching the Amish themselves. Once the play was written and the characters firmly established, I included details about the shooting that I felt would strengthen the texture of the play.

The fiction: I was highly aware through the entire process that somewhere out there are the real people who went through this event – the widow of the Nickel Mines gunman and her children, the Amish families of the girls who were targeted in the shooting...In an effort to balance the conflicting desires to remain sensitive to the real people who were affected by the shooting, while giving myself creative license to write an unflinching play, I purposefully did not research the gunman or his widow, nor did I conduct any interviews of any kind. The characters in *The Amish Project* are fictional, and should not be misconstrued as the real people.

The play: July 28th, 2008, my director and I traveled to Nickel Mines to find the location of the shooting. We had read that without an informed guide, it was nearly impossible to find, as shortly after the event the Amish tore down the school and replanted the area so that it is now a simple field where animals graze. The only indications of where the shooting occurred are three maple trees.

As we drove through the small intersection of farmland that is Nickel Mines, I realized that every person we saw, gardening or hanging clothes on the line, had likely grieved the loss of a child or the children of friends...As the sun was setting and we stood quietly looking at the three maple trees and the vacant space where they used to shade the one room schoolhouse, I could feel the tragedy that had occurred here, but even more I could feel the presence of those we had passed en route, the people who carry the memory of that day with them....

It is my private prayer that this play, should they ever know about it, would not hurt them further, but somehow honor the goodness they forged in the face of such tragedy. In my mind, that is the legacy of the Nickel Mines shooting.

– Jessica Dickey

A very special thank you is due to the following individuals:

To Jerry Richardson and my family (especially my parents Barry and Sarie Dickey), whose support cannot be measured; my tireless champion Morgan Jenness, and her assistant Micah Bucey; David Van Asselt, Brian Long, Daniel Talbott, Denis Butkus, Julie Kline, and all the rockstars at Rattlestick; Angelina Fiordellissi and the Cherry Lane Theatre; Elena Holy and the New York International Fringe Festival; Ben Sands and David Krasner of The Mine; The New Harmony Project; New Georges; Wendy Vanden Heuval; Geoff and Teresa Needham; Howard Leggett; Drs. Greg and Diana Lyon-Loftus and the members of Waynesboro Trinity Church; Willy Holtzman; Cameron and Einar Sunde; The Spiegler Trust; Jeff McCloud; Dr. Gladys Foxe. Also to my talented production team, Sarah Cameron Sunde, Lauren Helpern, Eugenia Furneaux-Arends, Nicole Pearce, Jill BC DuBoff, Dustin O'Neill, Lillian Vince, Kelly Schaffer, Natalie Robin, photographer Geoff Green; also Emily Ballou, Austin Bunn, and Emily Bohannon. And finally, to the many who donated to *The Amish Project*– it could never have been done without you.

Thank you!

–Jessica Dickey

(From the darkness:)

CAROL. Man Enters Amish Schoolhouse And Opens Fire.

(Lights up to reveal **VELDA***, a young Amish girl in the ethnic garb of her people – blue cotton dress, black stockings and shoes, a white apron and white bonnet.)*

VELDA. The best letter to write is lowercase f.

The long swirls.

Capital Gs are hard.

And capital Is.

I like lowercase f…and lowercase k.

Wanna hear a trick my teacher Miss Emma taught us?

Lowercase k actually looks like a kangaroo.

(She draws a very large lowercase k into the air with her finger.)

See, this is the mommy's body, and this is the baby in her pouch.

She's a marsupial.

And these are her long feet that help her jump.

And this is her big long tail…

Here, let's draw a hat on her, like Papa's.

(She draws the hat on the kangaroo and smiles.)

I'm always adding hats.

This is where I lost a tooth last week.

Guess what this is…

(She draws.)

Um, this is my Mama, and this is my Papa.

He really wears a hat.

My Mama wears a bonnet, like this.

(She draws the bonnet.)

Like this!

(She points to her own bonnet on her head.

She continues drawing.)

VELDA. *(cont.)* And this is our horse Cisco, he pulls the buggy,
and this is our cat Beesley,
and this is my brother Jacob,
and my little brother Elam...

And this is my sister Anna.
She has long hair the color of corn, and pink finger-nails.
And stinky feet.
And pretty pink lips.

ANNA. The first thing I see is flowers.
Flowers in the bright day yard behind our house.
And then my Papa working in the field, over and
beyond the hill.
I'm like a bird.
I can see where his shirt is a darker blue from his sweat.
And the dark circle of his hat.
Then suddenly I'm in the kitchen with my Mama.
She's sewing.
And she's humming.
Mama only hums when she doesn't know you're there,
but she has a nice voice.
The shadow in the room casts a long, brown blanket
over her,
hiding the little mole on her neck, right where her
dress starts.
I always touch it when I stand next to her at the table.
She is sewing the final squares on a quilt,
maybe for the new baby in the Zook family.
Blue squares with black and white triangles, rows and
rows of stitches.
She shifts in her chair and I see her little mole.

I reach out to touch it and she gasps.

And then suddenly I'm in the fields again,

but it's dark.

The moon is out.

I recognize the pump next to the schoolhouse by our farm,

but the school isn't there.

Just a dark square.

(Transition: **CAROL**, *early thirties, smoking a cigarette. She stares at the audience, watching them watch her, then...)*

CAROL. TV sucks.

I mean, really, it sucks.

Sometimes in the afternoon I'll turn it on, just for a change, you know,

and all the colors and fake people are like a rope around my neck.

There's men talking about cars

and women talking about women,

and someone is wiping a countertop,

and someone is eating bugs with a helmet on,

and a middle-aged couple is taking a pill

so "the moment" lasts

but go to the emergency room if

"the moment" lasts

more than four hours.

Literally my airway tightens.

The news is the worst.

Something bad happens and you can see them salivating.

Literally, the newscasters, frothing at the mouth.

"This just in!"

We don't watch TV anymore.

CAROL. *(cont.)* I was in the grocery store this morning and
It occurred to me for the first time…

I was in the hygiene aisle or whatever,

trying to find a moisturizer with the um, SPF or whatever…

No one tells you that even when you're mourning, you still worry about wrinkles.

So now you know.

So I'm reading the labels about the UVA and the UVB and

wham.

Just like that.

I think,

Just because it's written on this label,

doesn't mean it's true.

Something can be written down,

FDA approved,

FBI protected,

and that don't make it *true.*

And I'm standing there suddenly aware of the thousands of promises all around me,

on every little bottle and box, usually in some bright color,

"Reduces wrinkles,"

"Prevents tartar,"

"Gives stronger bones" –

and I think, it's all bullshit.

You can put your hand on a Bible and swear to tell the truth, and still lie.

The *Bible.*

And then you think, well what is the Bible?

How is that any different from the bright yellow words on the cover of my Advil that says

"Eliminates pain"?

The Bible: "Proof of God."

Really?

Is that where we got this whole God thing?

The Bible?

And then there's things that *are true.*

Now *that* is some sick shit.

The Bible has some true stuff in it...

people bein' nailed to crosses?!!

What the f – ?!!

Think of the sickest thing you've ever read.

Right now, do it.

It was *true,* wasn't it?

It was something that really happened.

What happens to a person when you live in a world

where you can't believe anything,

and the things you don't want to believe

are actually true?

You can swear in front of everyone you have ever known

that this person –

this person before you –

is The One.

You promise to stand by them and love them,

and nurse them and give them pleasure,

and let them nurse you and give you pleasure...

Right there – cheap tux, white dress, *swear*

in front of your family and friends.

Don't make it true.

VELDA. Soon will be Anna's Rumspringa.

That's when she has to decide whether or not to join
the Church.

Some don't, but most do, and if they don't,

we don't speak to them.

During Anna's Rumspringa

She's allowed to wear make-up and say cuss words and
kiss boys.

And she can't get in trouble for it.

I ask Anna everyday if she'll go far away for Rumspringa and she says she won't,

but I'm not sure.

For MY Rumspringa I'm going to go to the beach because I'm going to wear a bathing suit.

A red one with flowers on it.

It will show my breasts a little

but not too much.

And a boy will fall in love with me, and I'll let him kiss me,

And eventually, like after a month, the boy will ask me to marry him and I'll say,

"I can't marry you because you're not Amish."

And he'll say, "Oh please please please!"

and I'll say *(with great flirtation)* "No no no!"

And he'll say "Oh please please please!"

and I'll say "Okay, but you have to become Amish,"

and he'll say "Okay."

And then I'll bring him home to meet my family and my friends

and he'll play with my brothers

and he'll meet Anna (but he won't talk to her that much),

and then he'll become Amish.

I can't wait to have breasts!

Cows have breasts with milk in them,

but that's not the same thing.

(Transition: **BILL NORTH**, *English scholar and friend of the Amish, leads a press conference.)*

BILL. Well, I guess we're about ready to get started here,

If everyone wants to grab their coffee and settle in.

I'd like to offer a special thanks to the folks here at the firehouse for having us,

For letting their place here be Grand Central this whole week.

We won't be here too long tonight,

it's been a long day for everyone,

So if everyone wants to grab their coffee and settle in

We'll get this, uh, press conference underway.

CAROL. *(As newscaster)* This just in!

Widow of crazed schoolhouse gunman

buys a lotion with an SPF.

Here at the BS Channel we have the exclusive interview.

Now Carol Stuckey, why did you choose a lotion with an SPF?

(As herself) Well Craig,

I realized if I'd taken better care of my skin and prevented wrinkles from my face,

maybe my husband wouldn't have tried to molest little Amish girls.

(Pause)

(As newscaster) Uh huh, and how do you like the SPF lotion so far?

(As herself) Oh, it's awesome.

My fine lines are significantly reduced,

and I love the smooth, greaseless finish.

BILL. You're probably wondering who the heck I am.

My name is Bill North.

I'm a professor of American religion at the local university here,

and a friend of Aaron Yoder here,

and many of the Amish families affected by this, uh, tragic event.

Aaron asked me to speak for them here today

about their ways

and naturally I accepted.

I've been studying and teaching Amish culture for over 25 years,

And I'm very grateful for the opportunity to help in any way that I can right now.

BILL. *(cont.)* We hope that by gathering here together in this private way,

and talking a little bit about the Amish and their uh, culture...

It'll answer some of your questions,

Like– how could the Amish forgive such a thing...

And more importantly it'll help us all to understand their need,

especially now,

for privacy.

Uh, Aaron,

Is there anything you want to add?

No?... Okay.

I've had the privilege of knowing Aaron here for many...

Well, over 30 years now...

So. Let's dive in, shall we?

You know,

This tragedy happened to a private people.

So you came here to help the Amish

or to print their story –

But see, that's a complicated thing right there.

You may or may not know this,

But while the Amish themselves are pacifists,

As a *people* they are certainly no strangers to violence.

The original Amish, the Anabaptists, fled to America from Europe in the 1700s.

This was to escape harsh persecution for their beliefs.

There are many stories of torture and executions –

And they've pretty much been tryin' to keep to themselves ever since.

VELDA. Guess what this is.

(She draws a large cross with a body on it, adding nails in the hands and feet.)

Can you guess?

It's Jesus.

BILL. I've spent a lot of time with Aaron's family over the
   years –
   I've known both of his daughters, Anna and Velda,
   since they were born,
   And both – exceptional little girls.
   Anna – very bright in her studies, often talked of
   becoming a teacher one day.
   Velda – also bright, often delightfully precocious.
   Uh, Aaron, do you mind if I share
   that little anecdote that Velda taught me last time?

   Velda taught me

   (He draws each letter.)

   That J stands for Jesus, who comes first.
   Y stands for You, who comes last,
   and the O stands for Others,
   who connect the two.
   Giving you JOY.

   (He chuckles gently.)

   I like that.
   Giving you JOY.

VELDA. It's Jesus.
   See,
   This is the cross, and these are his hands and his feet.
   He has nails in them.
   Um, one time I got a nail in my hand because I was
   playing with the wood by the barn.
   I was trying to make a pen so my brother could be my
   piggy
   and I got a nail in my hand.
   We had to clean it.
   It hurt so much.
   It was right in the middle of my hand like Jesus.
   I said to my Mama, it's like Jesus.
   And she said,

   (her mother's voice)

VELDA. *(cont.)* Ja, verletze er.

> *(Returns to her own voice)*

Jesus hurt for us.

> *(VELDA adds a thorny crown.)*

And this is his hat.

Only Jesus really had a hat.

A very special one.

BILL. I'm assuming

You are all by and large strangers to this area...

You'll see that it is a very peaceful, beautiful country-side.

I hope you'll spend time in our local restaurants,

See some of the local sights...

I'm sure you'll also spend time learning about

What happened here this week,

But I hope you'll look for more than that.

There is more to here

Than what happened on October 2nd.

> *(Transition: SHERRY LOCAL, Non-Amish woman in her 50s)*

SHERRY LOCAL. We moved to Nickel Mines about 20 years ago,

Me and m' husband Ray.

We have a little farm 'bout 4 miles out of town,

And I work at the church part time in the office there.

On October 2nd, 2006, I was in m' basement,

Walkin' on our treadmill.

We keep it in the basement and

I usually watch the news while I

"walk it out"...

I read the headline across CNN –

Man Enters Amish Schoolhouse And Opens Fire.

I lost my footing on the treadmill and fell off,
Like something you'd see in a Jim Carey movie.

They kept showing these images over and over again –
It was a birds eye view:
Amish families gathering in a green field,
Clusters of men and women, boys and girls, separate,
but close.
The white ambulances with red lights,
Circled around the white schoolhouse.
Tiny rectangles of bodies covered in sheets.
The ticker tape running below –
Man Enters Amish Schoolhouse And Opens Fire
Man Enters Amish Schoolhouse And Opens Fire

Then the shocking details began to emerge.
This just in:
He was the local milkman.
He only shot the girls.
At least three dead.

Then the images again –
A birds eye
Amish families.
Separate, but close.
White ambulances.
White schoolhouse.
Bodies covered in sheets.
Man Enters Amish Schoolhouse And Opens Fire
Man Enters Amish Schoolhouse And Opens Fire

This just in:
He intended to molest them.
He shot himself.
Death toll now six.

Birds eye
Amish families.

SHERRY LOCAL. *(cont.)* Separate, but close.

> White ambulances.
> White schoolhouse.
> Bodies covered in sheets.
> Man Enters Amish Schoolhouse And Opens Fire.

> This just in:
> The Amish request that the medical condition of the remaining girls be withheld.
> They extend **forgiveness** to the gunman.
> They extend **condolences** to the gunman's family.

> Birds eye.
> Green field.
> Separate, but
> Close.
> White. Red.
> White.

> I thought –
> What kind of SICKO could do this?!!

CAROL. The boys seem kind of numb.

> I sometimes think *they're* the ones who are dead.
> They move around the house so quiet, sort of half-lit.
> The way they sit at the table, slumped over, spooning their cereal.
> Little ghosts.

> And then suddenly I'm painfully aware of how *alive* they are.
> I can see the veins beneath their skin,
> picture their little lungs, their little hearts,
> pumping blood, oxygen, every moment,
> right inside their little chests, right across the table.

> They've learned to trust only each other now.
> They don't dare cling to me the way they used to.
> Maybe *I'm* the ghost.

I'm sure if I could see me, I'd be scared too.

I keep my expectations low.

That they sit at the table and eat their cereal, that's enough.

That somehow I managed to put two bowls, two spoons,

a box of Frosted Flakes, that's Joshy's favorite,

a box of Cocoa Puffs, that's Jeremy's favorite,

on the table with milk, and they sit and eat it, and somehow get out the door to the carpool for the sitters,

is a miracle to me.

A total miracle.

That's a laugh –

I'm talkin' about miracles.

You wanna hear a miracle?

I still love my husband…

I miss him.

Last night I could have sworn he was standing on the lawn.

I got up and looked out the window,

middle of the night,

and could have sworn he was standing there,

just at the edge of the lawn, where the grass meets the road,

standing there.

I covered my eyes and said,

Go Away.

And when I looked again,

he was gone.

ANNA. Sir, please shoot me first.

VELDA. Please, shoot me second.

BILL NORTH. Okay, first of all, you need to understand
Most people think that Amish is just Amish, that they're all alike,

BILL NORTH. *(cont.)* But see, that's not exactly true.

Some Amish use a computer for business (battery powered),

some don't.

Some Amish have a phone at the end of their lane,

some don't...

So while on this side of the cultural fence the Amish appear "all alike"

(via their common symbols,

such as bonnets and buggies),

the truth is there are infinite variables in how each district negotiates being Amish in a modern world.

But all Amish do have a basic code of living,

and they call that the Ordnung.

And the basic foundation of the Ordnung,

can best be summed up by the Pennsylvania Dutch word

Uffgeva,

To give up.

See, the Amish give up their individual needs to the community.

This is their

JOY.

VELDA. Our ancestors were Martyrs.

You're a Martyr if you're killed for your beliefs.

BILL NORTH. Separation from Us

Has been their most successful means of survival, really.

VELDA. This is my favorite story from the *Martyrs Mirror.*

Um,

Dirk Willems was caught and convicted because he didn't believe

that you should be baptized as a little baby.

And the judge said,

(She takes on a judge voice.) Do you believe in baptizing little babies?

(As herself) And Dirk Willems said,

(She takes on Dirk Willem's voice.) No I don't.

(As herself) And the judge said,

(Judge voice) Then you're going to jail to be tortured and killed.

(As herself) And Dirk Willems said

(Dirk Willems) Okay.

(As herself) So they put Dirk Willems in a tower in a big castle surrounded by a moat.

But he was SO smart that he tied together a bunch of rags and made a rope

and snuck out the window and landed on the frozen ice on the moat

and he crossed and started to run away.

But a guard from the tower saw him escaping.

So he followed him down the rope

but when HE landed on the ice he was so FAT from being a guard that he fell through.

So the FAT guard called out

(She takes on the fat guard voice)

"Help help!"

(As herself)

And Dirk Willems heard his cry and didn't know what to do.

But when he saw that the FAT guard was going to drown

He went back and pulled him from the icy water and saved his life.

But then the FAT guard arrested Dirk Willems

And threw him back in jail

where he was burned at the stake.

*(Transition: **AMERICA**, sixteen and pregnant)*

AMERICA. I work here at the Giant Food on Route 30,
    That's how I know the crazy guy's wife.

AMERICA. *(cont.)* Okay, I know what you're thinking.

You're thinking,

She don't belong here!

Am I right?

You're thinking,

Oh, there are other "other people" in Lancaster besides the Amish?

The answer is – yeah!

My mother is Puerto Rican and I was born here.

She got pregnant with me as soon as she got here and that's why she named me

America.

She was two years older than me when she got pregnant.

I'm sixteen.

Okay, I know what you're thinking –

Sixteen and pregnant! She's a slut.

Am I right?

That's what my mother said:

She said,

(Her mother's voice)

I don't work at a filthy chicken factory

Everyday for sixteen years

so my daughter can be a cliché.

(Back to her own voice)

Okay, she read that word in her Reader's Digest, I know it.

I said, Don't quote your Reader's Crygest to me.

My father was some black guy she dated in New York and then he dumped her when she got pregnant.

But Demetrius is the only one I ever been with,

So I can't be a slut.

Okay,

I know what you're thinking –

Demetrius like in A Midsummer's Night Dream!
Am I right?!!
We read that play in English this year, by Mr. William
Shakespeare.
I played Titania!
Titania is totally fierce!
She's like, all beautiful and sassy,
And she's got her man but she's still independent.
It was good casting.
I'm thinking about doing my Titania speech for the
Mother-Daughter night at school next month.
You're supposed to have something memorized to
recite.

Demetrius and I might get married but I don't know.
We haven't figured that out yet.
He AIN'T gonna dump me.
Okay,
I know it's a sin.
I'm a Catholic.
Wait – is it a cliché if I'm a Catholic?
I don't even care cuz if you saw Demetrius
you would understand.
He's got these big lips that he licks all the time.
He makes me crazy!
I'm like, Demetrius you lickin' those lips and makin'
me crazy!
He just laughs and slaps my butt.

Okay, I know you're thinking,
Oh, her and Demetrius gonna have her baby and live
off her mother's minimum wage,
But I ain't. I got a job.
I work here at the Giant Food on Route 30.

Nobody can tell yet. I just look like I had a lot of
lasagna.

AMERICA. *(cont.)* Oh, what–? You thought I was gonna say tacos?!!

Am I right?

No way, I love me some LASAGNA!

BILL NORTH. A perfect example are the barn raisings that the Amish are so known for.

When it's time for a raising in Amish land,

it's like a home football game for us.

Everyone comes, people cook and eat, there's enthusiasm and comradery.

Except that instead of watching the players do something for its own sake,

Amish fun involves everyone chipping in to make something useful for a neighbor.

Same with the way the women quilt.

See, they don't separate work and leisure like we do.

CAROL. Oh hell

Eddie and I met at a church gathering,

if you can believe that.

Not our church, of course – neither of us ever went in for that...

I mean, my parents took me when I was little, but –

No – we was both there with other people.

I was there with my friend Karen Woodring,

and Eddie was with his girlfriend Kathy.

I forget her last name.

Kathy was a nice girl.

Dumb as a rock.

Had huge boobs.

Just huge.

I guess we sort of knew each other, the way everybody knows each other in a small town.

I'd been workin' in my Dad's store since I was eleven and I'd seen him come in and out over the years, but we'd never talked, and I was younger than him in school.

Anyway, at some point Kathy and Karen and all the other youth group kids

had to go have a meeting or whatever,

and Eddie and I sat on the swing set.

Smoked and talked.

And something just – clicked.

He broke up with Kathy and her huge boobs that night.

AMERICA. Telling my mother was the worst.

Last night

We was picking out our outfits for the Mother-Daughter night at school.

She was digging through the closet and I told her.

She slapped my face.

She said I'd better look to Saint Francis now,

Only Saint Francis would help me.

Fuck her!

CAROL. He wrote

"Dear Carol.

I'm sorry that I won't see the boys grow up.

You're a good mother and I know it will be hard for you now.

I hope you can forgive me for that.

Please understand and try to forgive me.

Tell the boys that I love 'em.

Tell 'em –

I wasn't all bad."

He never did write all that well.

Usually just signed his name on things.

Last year I opened my birthday card and he wrote,

I love you, honey.

I about fell out of my chair.

(Transition: **EDDIE** *watches the audience watch him.*
Then –)

EDDIE. I'll tell ya right now, I'm ain't gonna say Why.
You don't get that.
You ain't gonna understand anyway, and –
I know – I know you're thinkin',
Oh was he molested? Or –
Oh was he possessed by the Devil
or whatever?
And – I just ain't gonna give it to ya.
So if you're still interested in listenin' –
I'll talk.
Cuz I'm more than that, you know –
I'm more than the Why…

(Transition)

SHERRY. If you were a decent wife
Those poor girls would be alive today.

CAROL. Some woman came up to me
in the grocery store, perfectly normal looking woman,
came up to me…
I was in the hygiene aisle,
reading the lies on some face lotion,
and this woman came up to me, put her cart next to
my cart and said,
If you were a decent wife
those poor girls would be alive today.
She said,

SHERRY LOCAL. There is a fresh hell
where you'll join
your SICKO husband.

CAROL. And for some reason
I laughed.
Oh, I ran to the parking lot, smeared moisturizer on
my face,
scratched myself over and over again,

But in the moment I laughed.

You do things like that when you're losin' your mind.

SHERRY LOCAL. Man Enters Amish Schoolhouse And Opens Fire.

AMERICA. Okay,

Titania's speech is like, totally smart.

She's all like, I'm the Fairy Queen, Oberon!

(As Titania)

These are the forgeries of jealousy.

(As herself)

Okay?

But then she talks about how the animals are messed up,

The crops are messed up,

Kids are old before their time,

All because her and Oberon are fighting.

I like that part,

Like it's from all of our fighting

that the world is messed up.

EDDIE. I like the kind of flowers that smell.

And the color blue.

I like to kiss Joshy and Jer on the top of their heads.

I like cats.

We can't have none on account of Carol bein' allergic,

and that's probably just as well cuz I don't like the litter boxes or whatever.

At the jewelry store in town that Joe Mitchell runs I got a ring I been payin' off slowly for Carol.

Whenever I can I'll just go in and just give him twenty bucks or so to put towards the ring.

With the kids and all we don't have too much extra,

but I know she likes nice things.

She deserves nice things.

CAROL. It was the word
>Sicko.
>Sicko.
>Sicko.
>Sicko. Sicko.
>Sickosickosickosickosickosickosickosicko.
>Sicko.
>Sicko.

AMERICA. Okay I decided to look at what Saint Francis wrote,
>Because my mother likes him.
>Saint Francis!!??– is totally different!
>Saint Francis says:
>For it is in giving
>that we receive,
>It is in pardoning,
>That we are pardoned.
>It is in dying,
>we are born to eternal life.

>That's DEEP, right?
>But Titania is so awesome.
>Which one am I gonna do?
>I really need my speech for the Mother-Daughter night to be GOOD.

EDDIE. When we was first dating,
>I was kind of a wild kid, I guess, and I was always tryin' to get her to come out late with me,
>after hours and all that.
>Her folks had a place on Davis Road,
>a little rancher that always smelled like pickles,
>and her bedroom was in the back facing the yard.
>Well I'd stand there out in her yard,
>'specially on a warm night,
>waitin' for her to look out and
>see me.

I know I could've walked up to the window and been
like,

Yo Carol,

but I don't know...

there was something about waiting for her to look out
and

see me.

(**VELDA** *draws.*)

VELDA. This is The Man. This is his hat.

SHERRY LOCAL. Man Enters –

EDDIE. I know – !

I know that magical things happen to people...

I mean, I never had nothin' magical happen to me
that I know of,

but I know that magical things do happen to people...

Like one time my buddy Troy,

his Dad once got a real bad feeling about their old
Chevy truck,

had a vision of broken glass or something,

so he parked it in the yard and told 'em they weren't
gonna drive it for a little while.

And then, like a week later, while they was at the movies,

this huge semi went off the highway,

this was over there by 272 –

flew right into their Chevy truck,

smashed it to pieces...

So, there's some kind of Somethin' that's out there.

But I've always thought that real magic happens on the
other side...

in the places we can't be,

the places that are protected from us...

AMERICA. Okay,

I have never met HIM, but I know his wife.

She's always shopped here, since I worked here anyway.

She's not that old –
Sometimes she'll have one of her kids with her,
But mostly she's by herself.
I've *never* seen her husband and thank God.
I would be scared of him.

So I passed her in the hygiene aisle,
And she was sort of staring at the shelves or reading or something.
And it was like she had this invisible thing on her
Like this invisible, heavy, soaked blanket around her neck,
Like hanging on her.
My mother calls that
La tristeza del mundo,
The sadness of the world.
Some people, you look at them, and you can see it.

I normally help customers find things
'cuz I'm good at it,
But I didn't try to talk to her.
I don't know why –
I guess I was scared, like maybe she was crazy too or something.
She always look like a normal white lady to me.
Just goes to show everybody's got problems –
Like some people are sixteen and pregnant,
Some people have daughters who are sixteen and pregnant,
Some people have crazy husbands.

CAROL. Sicko.
Sicko.
Sickosickosickosickosickosickosickosicko.
Sickosickosickosickosickosickosickosicko soickosicko.

Sicko.

Sicko.

There's a fresh hell

where you'll join

your sicko husband.

I'm sure she's right.

SHERRY LOCAL. Oh I ain't proud of it but come on now,

You was thinkin' it too.

You been seein' it on the news –

these pitchers of the schoolhouse and the Amish in their buggies,

But to be here, where it all happened, and see those poor people...

I mean, the Amish may have their *WAYS* –

they ain't *normal*, that's clear –

but you can see they're good people.

AMERICA. Oh I seen the whole thing.

This fat woman went up to her in the grocery store and said something to her,

Not real loud or anything,

But I could tell it was bad

'cuz she ran out!

The crazy guy's wife ran out!

SHERRY LOCAL. Believe me,

I ain't never said somethin' so mean in my entire life.

But all day I'd been watchin' the news and feelin' so sick 'n' sad,

and I saw her there in the grocery store, and somethin' just snapped.

It's like my mother always said

that she would hate Mr. Meisner til she was dead.

Now Mr. Meisner was my math teacher that touched me in a mean way when I was 'bout 13,

And I told my mother and she told the principal and he didn't believe her.

SHERRY LOCAL. *(cont.)* Just didn't believe her.

So she told me she knew I had to be nice to Mr. Meisner
'cuz he was m' teacher,

But that not to worry,

SHE would hate him enough

for the BOTH of us...

You get what I'm tellin' you?

So it's easier for the Amish to do their

We forgive him thing

If WE carry that, you know?

If WE hold on.

Don't get me wrong –

The Amish ain't exactly innocent.

You don't watch TV or read the paper,

You're practically makin' yourself a target,

And there ain't a man alive who don't hate goin'
around them damn buggies.

How many accidents a year do that cause?

And don't even get my husband Ray on the subject cuz
he will give you a right earful.

Most of the farmers in the area hate the Amish –

Because we're workin' so hard just to pay the bills

And they're rollin' in it,

All 'cuz they're willing to make their kids work

And we pay for big farm equipment –

Oh, don't get me started!

So I ain't exactly stickin' up for the Amish, but we gotta
draw the line somewhere.

I mean, can you imagine –

Oh that's alright, Sicko!

You just go right ahead, do whatever you want, we'll
FORGIVE YA.

What's that say to all the other Sickos?!!

And don't tell me a WIFE don't know
SOMETHIN' like THAT!

AMERICA. I ran out after her.

I don't know what I thought I was going to do,

I found her in the parking lot.

She was crouched down between some cars, smearing moisturizer on her face, her face all red.

I didn't know what to say.

She looked like an animal.

I said,

Ma'am, are you okay?

Are you okay?

She said,

CAROL. You know what – why don't you fuck off –

FUCK OFF, TACO.

(Transition)

EDDIE. I used to watch 'em while I did my rounds.

You ever seen 'em?

I mean, a whole flock of 'em –

in a field or crossing the road?

Their little legs

in their stockings,

the little bib things they wear,

the way their hair twists up and disappears into their little bonnets…

it's like – all that beauty,

all that pink,

tucked away under there,

hidden.

Like a clean secret.

They sort of scatter as you come near.

But once in a while if you wave,

one of 'em will wave back.

*(**EDDIE** waves to **ANNA**.)*

*(Transition: **ANNA** waves back.)*

ANNA. He came into the school while Miss Emma was preparing the blackboard for a spelling exercise.

We are seated at our desks, so he seems very tall.

He asks if we've seen a clevis pin he'd lost along the road.

I know what a clevis pin is because of my father's farm equipment.

We say we haven't seen it.

He doesn't look anyone in the eye.

CAROL. "Visibly reduces wrinkles."

"Fades dark circles and smoothes fine lines."

"Helps you shave less often."

SHERRY LOCAL. Man Enters Amish Schoolhouse…

ANNA. When he comes back, he has a gun.

He makes the boys and Miss Emma leave.

He barricades the front door.

He tells the girls to line up along the chalkboard.

There are ten of us.

He ties our wrists with plastic ties, and our feet.

As he ties my wrists, I can smell him.

He doesn't smell bad, maybe like soap,

but I can tell how hard he's breathing.

I can see sweat on his chin.

I think of my Papa, how I've never seen his chin.

(VELDA draws.)

VELDA. This is The Man.

This is his hat.

This is his gun.

He said, Pray for me.

CAROL. "Cuts through tough soap scum fast."

"Soothes as it heals."

"Instant relief that lasts for hours."

"Blocks pain."

ANNA. I started praying to God,
trying to feel how God would want me to behave
but my heart is racing,
the air feels like wool.
He looks at me.

VELDA. Anna is looking at the man,
But I want her to look at me.
She is looking at the man
But I want her to look at me!

CAROL. "Seek and ye shall find."
"The meek shall inherit the earth."
"New and improved lemony scent."

ANNA. Some of the littler girls don't really understand English yet,
and they're talking quietly in our language.
But he doesn't seem to notice because the police are pulling up around the school.
Everything is getting louder and louder –
he yells out at the police
and they order him with their
microphone thing.

CAROL. And forgive us our trespasses,
as we forgive those who trespass against us...

ANNA. Sweat pours down his face.
I can see where his shirt
is darker from his sweat.
He keeps looking at me,
then back at the police.
They scream at him,
He screams back.
His fingers twitching on the gun.
We are lined up against the chalkboard,
Wanting our mamas.
Waiting.

CAROL. And deliver us from Evil –

EDDIE. I wanted to have the girls.

CAROL. For thine is the kingdom,
the power,
and the glory,
for ever and ever.

EDDIE. I wanted to have the girls!
But the police arrived real fast –
I don't know how – so fast –
I didn't get to have the girls.
So I shot 'em.

ANNA. Sir, please shoot me first!

VELDA. Please, shoot me second!

EDDIE. I shot 'em!
Each one.
In the head.
Then I shot myself.

(Transition: **VELDA** *sings an Amish hymn.)*

VELDA. O God our Father
O Open me
With your love
Teach me to forgive
With your love

SHERRY LOCAL. Man Enters –

VELDA. – Amish –

ANNA. – Schoolhouse –

CAROL. ...And Opens Fire.

(Transition)

Got back from the store,
Moisturizer still wet on my face,
And the Amish were here.
Spent all morning with me.
There were about five of 'em here, huddled here
together in the living room...

CAROL. *(cont.)* I was shocked to see them.

I mean, shocked they were *here,*

And then shocked because, well,

They're *shocking.*

They're freaks.

They have a weird smell.

Not bad, really, just weird.

The women wear those bonnets and cotton dresses,

And the men have the blue shirts with suspenders and hats.

Like another planet.

He sat there *(She motions to the chair.)*

His name was Aaron.

BILL. The Amish don't normally accept charity.

They rarely even use social security or government programs like that.

But given the extent –

the scope of this has exceeded the community fund the Amish have for difficult times.

And so they accept your donation.

I'm sure they'd like me to extend their thanks.

Aaron has told me that they intend to use the money for all of the victims,

including the gunman's widow and her two children.

Aaron and some of the other Amish parents visited with Mrs. Stuckey earlier this morning.

Many of my students have been asking

the same thing you've been asking,

How could the Amish

Forgive such a thing?

And yes – of course – yes –

And why…

WHY would someone do this?

Why would –

But the Amish believe –

BILL. *(cont.)* And – please – this is very important –
      That there is no WHY.
      That even if we could be inside Edward Stuckey's mind
      as he drove up to the schoolhouse, as he –
      We would still never really understand…

CAROL. They brought food –
      I haven't even really had a chance to look and see what
      all they brought.
      Maybe there were more than five, it's hard to recall
      exactly.
      He's the only one I really remember.
      He sat there.
      It's odd, the way they wear their beards…
      Eddie never wore a beard.
      It was always slow to grow, even after a week.
      They don't have the moustache part, you know.
      I think it's the married men who have the beards.
      Someone once told me they don't wear the moustache
      On account that that used to be associated with the
      military or something, way back when,
      but I don't know if that's true.
      A man's upper lip is such a strange spot…

      I sat there looking at him,
      his blond beard,
      a little red in it once the sun was full coming in the
      window,
      the pink of his upper lip,
      his pink fingernails, scrubbed clean.

      What he and his wife must have been through.
      What his little girls must have been through.

ANNA. I guess most of all I'll miss my family.
      I'll miss the taste of Mama's peach jam.
      I'll miss barn parties.
      I don't know if you know this,

ANNA. *(cont.)* but we can have *serious* parties sometimes.

They can get crazy.

I love to dance! I love it.

I love it when the music is so loud you can feel it in your chest.

CAROL. Did I tell you they brought food?

I haven't had a chance to see what all they brought.

Some of 'em sat down here with me and then a few of 'em,

I guess it must've been the women,

went right to the kitchen

and I could vaguely hear them opening the fridge and putting things in.

I wished I'd have known they were comin';

I'd have read up a bit.

Do they even have fridges?

Well they must, right?

I know some of 'em use more modern appliances than the others.

Like some of 'em have phones,

but I don't think in the house or whatever.

I don't think they use electricity.

So how could they have a fridge?

They were very polite.

They kept deferring to me, to my grief.

I wanted to say, stop.

Stop.

They talk so slowly and so quietly.

I kind of like that.

Like being read to sleep or something.

I just tried not to cuss.

At one point I saw something move outside and I thought it might be Eddie.

It was one of their horses parked in the driveway.

A horse

CAROL. *(cont.)* in my driveway.

> I about laughed out loud.
>
> I asked him what farm they live on and he said the one on Stultz Road.
> I know that farm.
> It's not far from the schoolhouse.
> It was on Eddie's route.
> I haven't been down that road since the boys were born, a good five, six years.
> I used to ride with Eddie on his route in the mornings when we was first married.
> I wanted to tell him that,
> the Amish man.
> About Eddie.
> But I didn't.

EDDIE. I like the kind of flowers that smell.

CAROL. I asked him how they were,

> how his
> little girls
> were…
>
> And he looked at me and said
>
> *(She gently takes on Aaron's voice)*
>
> We must trust in God now.
>
> *(back to her own voice)*
>
> Is that right?
> Trust in God.
>
> I love that.
> I love when people say that shit.
> Have you turned on the TV lately?
> Oh you haven't?
> You don't believe in TV?
> Well isn't that nice for you.
> Lemme fill you in:
> Shit like this happens everyday.

Shit
that is this sick *and more,*
happens every fuckin' day.
And the scary thing is,
as mortified as I am by my husband's actions –
the man that I swore in front of all my friends and
family
to go through my life as ONE –
as *disgusting* –
Eddie wasn't a bad guy.
He wasn't the Devil.
He just couldn't keep his darkness down anymore,
and it ate him.
It ate him
and it ate those poor little girls,
and now it's eating me.
And you can pull your hat down and say that's Evil
but the truth is –
that's all of us.
That's the world.
We're all just a few bad days from SICKO
and that's not Satan, that's the truth.
It lives in me
and yes, it lives in you.

And if your God –

SHERRY LOCAL. – Man Enters–!

CAROL. – is so fucking great –

SHERRY LOCAL. – Amish Schoolhouse–!

CAROL. – then where was He?!!

SHERRY LOCAL. – And Opens Fire–!

CAROL. Where was your God
        when my husband took three guns,
        KY Jelly and plastic ties
        and drove over to Stultz Road?

CAROL. *(cont.)* You know you show up here, try to make
nice with the Sicko's wife,
Well now you know.
Now you see what I am. You can leave.

Amish people putting food in my fridge,
That poor girl at the store tried to help me and
I was such a fuckin' bitch to her.
I wanted to rip my skin off.
I said YOU CAN GET OUT!

And then –
right then– he looks at me.
He looks right at me,
with his weird beard
and his blue eyes,
and there –, right there –,
in the middle of his eyebrows, is a –
Word.
One Word.
And he pushes that Word
into my brain
with his blue stare.

(Transition)

BILL NORTH. When I was a sophomore at Elizabethtown
College,
Just down the road here,
I was driving around looking for a barbecue that my
friend was having at his parents' house...
And somehow I'd gotten disoriented on the back
roads, and I was trying to –
I don't know how it happened, to this day –
But he came out of nowhere,
On his uh –

(He mimes pushing a scooter with his leg.)
Scooter –

blond hair, about 8 years old.
My little Honda Civic knocked him – twenty feet.

I remember the shock of him against the grey road –
His bright hair,
his blue shirt,
his yellow hat
next to his red blood…

CAROL. You would think if you're a lowly sack of shit
it'd be pretty great to have an angel sit in your living
room.
Not so much.
To feel like your whole being is a rotting grave,
and have this –
man flower –
sit with you,
BE with you…
hurts.
It hurts so much.
But it also helps.
In a way that nothing else –

BILL. I was sitting in the Emergency Room,
Not a scratch on me but – I was a mess –
I remember his parents held me –
The stranger who had run over their son –
They held me as I cried.
They kept saying –

(Gently takes on their voice)

It's alright,
It's alright,
It's alright.

(Back to his own voice)

Heavy to receive,
And heavy to give.

CAROL. And the Word,
> that word…
> It's like he burned it there,
> burned it with his face
> into my face.
> That Word repeats itself
> over and over
> in my mind.

AMERICA. I know what you're thinking –
> Taco.
> Slut.
> Cliché.
> Cliché.

> *(VELDA draws.)*

VELDA. This is Anna, with her pretty pink lips.
> These are the ties on her wrists and feet.
> And the bullet.

ANNA. The first thing I see is flowers.
> Flowers in the bright day yard behind our house.

BILL. After a long battle,
> Aaron did eventually fully recover –
> And he has been my friend
> ever since.

> *(Transition)*

CAROL. Every night, after I put the boys to bed,
> I drive over to Stultz Road.
> I park the car at the end of the dirt lane
> walk the quarter mile to his yard,
> and stand before his door, feeling him on the other side.
> The house is usually dark,
> they go to bed so much earlier than we do,
> but sometimes I see him in there,
> see him burdened by the sadness of the world…

ANNA. It's one of those beautiful Fall nights
　　when the moon is full and you can see for miles.
　　Everything is deep blue.
　　The lamp is burning in our kitchen.
　　I can see my Papa.
　　He can't sleep again.
　　I see the bald spot at the top of his head,
　　the way the skin is pink and shiny there.
　　I go to kiss it, but suddenly
　　He puts his head against the table
　　and squeezes his arms around his face and shoulders.
　　He doesn't want to wake Mama.
　　Deep sobs.
　　He sounds like an animal,
　　like there's an animal inside him trying to get out.
　　I see his body in the fight, muscles tight, shaking.
　　His hand is on his heart, and he's muttering over and
　　over…

　　(She gently takes on his voice.)

　　Help me, Lord. Help me.

　　(Back to her own voice)

　　Then suddenly I'm back into the night air.
　　I'm like a bird.
　　I look down and there is someone standing in our yard.
　　A woman.
　　She is standing in our yard.
　　She is watching Papa.
　　Then I'm off.

CAROL. And then I go home.
　　I go back to bed.
　　And the next day is easier.
　　Easier because –
　　He exists.

BILL. There is something about Them…

Something that unsettles you.

I've been teaching about Them, studying Them for 25 years –

It doesn't matter what your faith is or if you even have one –

Something about them makes you wonder –

What Am I?

Could I Be –

More?

VELDA. Um, one time when Anna had the flu,

Marian and I put some peach jam on a piece of bread, wrapped it in a towel,

and threw it up into Anna's bedroom window.

To cheer her up.

It was spring so the window was open, and Marian

Just threw it with all her might,

and it went right through the window!

It landed right on Anna's bed!

We couldn't believe it!

We could hear Anna laughing and coughing,

So we knew she'd gotten it.

(**VELDA** *draws Marian.*)

This is Anna's best friend, Marian.

AMERICA. I got back from the Mother-Daughter night.

It was tonight.

My mother didn't come.

So I went, but as a mother,

And my daughter was inside me.

I did do Saint Francis.

Maybe I'll do Titania next year.

But when I got home, the white lady was sitting on the couch

With my mother.

AMERICA. *(cont.)* My mother was crying.

My mother said, Siéntate, bebé.

So I sat down on the couch.

The white lady said,

I was just telling your mother

That you tried to help me at the store.

The white lady said,

She was sorry.

She said to my mother, and then to me,

I was a good girl.

VELDA. This is my best friend Emma.

She has red hair and she can hold her breath a LONG time.

(She continues to draw each girl.)

This is Margaret.

Um – She has the weirdest teeth.

CAROL. Last night, I saw Eddie.

Saw him standing out on the lawn,

right where the grass meets the road.

I don't know how long he'd been standin' there,

waitin' for me to look out and

see him.

I couldn't see his face, of course, it was too dark,

But I knew it was him.

I go to the window and look out.

I don't know how long for.

But I look at him,

and there it is –

The Word – that Word –

I send that Word to Eddie.

Just stare at him and repeat it over and over,

sort of beggin' him, sort of reassurin' him.

Until eventually, I see him fade.

See him fade into the night.

Until he's gone.

CAROL. *(cont.)* And then I'm soaring over the fields.
  I'm like a bird.

VELDA. This is Catherine.
  She's a great singer.

CAROL. I swoop down into a barn and there is music,
  A music I can feel inside my chest.
  And I feel all light and pink.

VELDA. This is Elizabeth
  Who talks ALL THE TIME,
  And her little sister Mary.
  Who never talks at all.
  And this is Dottie.
  She snorts when she laughs.
  And then– there's Little Esther.

CAROL. Suddenly I swoop back into the sky,
  And fly right toward this huge-ass moon.
  This huge-ass white moon
  in the middle of the bright day sky.
  And I feel so light,
  Like I am *meant* to fly to the moon,
  Like that's what I am made for.

(**VELDA** *counts down the line of her drawings of the girls, pointing at each one, like a gunshot…*)

VELDA. One!
  Two!
  Three!
  Four!
  Five!
  Six!
  Seven!
  Eight!
  Nine!

(*She takes her place inside her drawing, holding her wrists and feet as if they're bound.*)

VELDA. *(cont.)* Ten.

> *(She looks intently at the audience.)*

Can you see Him?
He's here.
God
is here.

Can you see Him?
Can you see Him?

Keep looking.

End of Play

OTHER TITLES AVAILABLE FROM SAMUEL FRENCH

TAKING FLIGHT

Adriana Sevahn Nichols

Dramatic Comedy / 1f

First there was Mary and Rhoda, then Thelma and Louise, and now Adriana and Rhonda, two loveable and unforgettable friends. One, searching for the goddess and her shamanic roots, the other, planning her epic "*Godfather* meets the *Mists of Avalon*" wedding, until 9/11 changes everything, leaving one in a hospital bed and the other intent on doing whatever it takes to save her friend. In this award winning play, "Sevahn Nichols joins the ranks of the best," (*SD Union Tribune*) as she takes you on a deeply moving, hilarious, and courageous journey into the depth of friendship, the challenge of care-giving, and the resilience of the human spirit.

Originally developed at the Sundance Theatre Lab, South Coast Repertory, and produced by Center Theatre Group at the Kirk Douglas Theatre, San Diego Rep, and the Goodman Theatre, this "enthralling play is an example of how good a one person show can be." *BackStage*) During the "80 minutes of tremendous theatre satisfaction," (*SD Theatre Scene*) you will discover why the heart is the strongest muscle we have in our bodies and experience why Pulitzer Prize winning playwright, Nilo Cruz, named *Taking Flight*, "a magnificent piece for the theatre…an allegory of our time."

"Brave Lady. Brave Tale. Brave Performance."
– *Daily News*

"Enthralling play…Sevahn-Nichols is a remarkable actor and storyteller. She flows seamlessly between portraying herself and the other character… Her strong charisma and her ability to keep the pace fast without feeling rushed are impressive. The tightly written script is honest and unafraid to jump radically from dark moments to humorous ones. The play is ultimately about not giving up…a celebration of life…and an example of how good a one person show can be. Kirk Douglas came onstage and praised her talent and her bravery. He was right on both accounts."
– *Back Stage*

OTHER TITLES AVAILABLE FROM SAMUEL FRENCH

BLUE YONDER

Kate Aspengren

Monologues & Scenes / Dramatic Comedy / 12 f (can be performed by 4f, or any number in between)

A familiar adage states, "Men may work from sun to sun, but women's work is never done." In *Blue Yonder*, the audience meets twelve mesmerizing and eccentric women including a flight instructor, a firefighter, a stuntwoman, a woman who donates body parts, an employment counselor, a professional softball player, a surgical nurse professional baseball player, and a daredevil who plays with dynamite among others. Through the monologues, each woman examines her life's work and explores the career that she has found. Or that has found her.

CPSIA information can be obtained at www.ICGtesting.com
Printed in the USA
LVOW130353130912

298518LV00005B/47/P